SILENT SCREAMS

Silent Screams
A View From The Soul's Edge

Ernest Federspiel

DEDICATIONS

Deuteronomy 28:34
"You shall be driven mad by the sight of what you see."

This book is dedicated to my three sons
Derek, Dylan, and Damon.
May you always find the love and peace of this life's journey while exploring the
unconventional aspects life has to offer. Keep your sanity safe and always take the
time to view all sides of a subject before making life-changing assumptions based on
false tales.
With unbound love, Dad

EPIGRAPH

"The unexamined life is not worth living."

Socrates

"Life should not be a journey to the grave with the intention of arriving safely in a pretty and well-preserved body, but rather to skid in broadside in a cloud of smoke, thoroughly used up, totally worn out, and loudly proclaiming
'Wow! What a Ride!'"

Hunter S. Thompson

Introduction

"Welcome, dear readers to Silent Screams: A View from the Soul's Edge.

Within the fractured mirror of the psyche, where perceptions distort and reality shatters, this book, Silent Screams, ignites a spark, a voice. It ventures into the abyss of insanity, where fantasies are unleashed, and the chains of reality melt away, freed by an altered imagination.

Embark on a journey through bent echoes from the soul's edge, where each poem challenges boundaries of sanity and invites you to explore uncharted territories of the human psyche. Open your mind and prepare to embrace the chaos within.

This book seeks to ignite your imagination, stir your thoughts, and offer a haven to find peaceful insanity. It is a whimsical journey into the realms of intrigue and fantasy, a deep dive into the serene madness of the mind."

Ernest Federspiel

Acknowledgments

Mike McArdle: "Mike, you're more than a brother; you've been my protector, my mentor, my confidant. Always an example of true strength and kindness. Our family bond, forged in shared experiences and unwavering support, is a treasure I hold dear. Love ya."

Neil Shanebeck: A lifelong brother who engaged in the unhinged path life took us on. 'One hell of a ride, Dawg'.

Greg Webster: A true brother who rode the edge of life with me, pushing every boundary. "Wild times, bro."

For the gracious testimonials provided:
Andy Christina Lopez-Villalobos
Laura Bennett: Author
Brad Sandlin: Author

SpillWords.com: A tremendous website showcasing a variety of poets.

Medusa's Kitchen.com: Another fantastic website that highlights poetry.

Canva Pro: A fantastic program I use to design and build my books and also for AI images.

I would also like to thank **Lightning Source LLC** for our business relationship and for providing the platform, resources, and fantastic support in bringing my books to life.

"To every soul, seen and unseen, including my brothers and sisters of the road: Your echoes have blessed my knowledge of life and made me who I am. May this work reflect that gift. With deepest gratitude."

Ernest Federspiel

Silent Screams
A View from the Soul's Edge
First Edition

Ernest Federspiel

The author owns all rights to previously published poems. They were published under non-exclusive rights [rights revert to the author upon publication].

Published by Peaceful Insanity Press

ISBN: 979-8-9913833-1-8

Disclaimer: This is a work of fiction. All poems, characters, and events in this book are products of the author's imagination. Any resemblance to actual persons, living or dead, or actual events is purely coincidental.[Unless otherwise noted].

Table Of Contents

Table of Contents
Silent Screams
A View from the Soul's Edge

Section One - Illusion Or Confusion

Section Two - Inside The Insanity

Table of Contents
Silent Screams
A View from the Soul's Edge

Section Two - Inside The Insanity

Table of Contents

Silent Screams
A View from the Soul's Edge

Section Two - Inside The Insanity

TABLE OF CONTENTS
SILENT SCREAMS
A VIEW FROM THE SOUL'S EDGE

SECTION TWO ~ INSIDE THE INSANITY

SECTION THREE ~ EDGE OF THE ABYSS

Silent Screams

A View From The Soul's Edge

Section One - Illusion Or Confusion

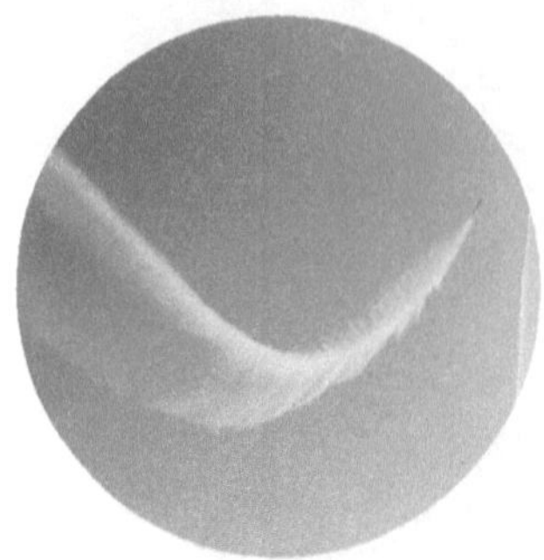

Like a jet stream leaving a trail in the sky
Thoughts in my mind leave a vapor of thought
Confused Confucius in rhyme

INDIA

Greenish-blue compost lay before the feet of twilight
As the blackness of midnight nightmares came to an end
When the eyes of India came slowly into focus
Slime-covered dreams remained solid refusing to bend

Screams arose deep inside not finding a passage out
They were forevermore trapped inside a terrified mind
A tragic story of how happiness eluded India
Refusing her the hope of letting her soul shine

The sky is spitting down on me
I woke up with this uneasy feeling
That peace I'll never see

I hear the thunder slowly rolling
Leaving destruction in it's path
Peaceful reflections

The sun dries the rain
Warmth covers the ground
Murder is rising

In a quicksand pit, the mind slowly is taken over by fear
With no way out, upon your cheeks flow stinging tears
No branches to pull yourself out, destined to sink
In this state of confusion, it's getting hard to think
Waist high now and soon it will reach the throat
One last wish is that you could enjoy some smoke
Tasting grit as the sand slowly enters your lips
I should have paid attention, now I'm in a world of shit

"ANGELS"

I believe in angels
How they protect us
From Ourselves

GOLDEN

Leaves on the trees turning golden
Life in a state of change
Cherry blossoms await

ONLY I KNOW

Dreams only I know
Clouds slowly rolling
Coffee steamed to delight

Came out as a rebel, with no rules to the games I played
The edge of disaster gave me the grin I wear today
A throttle in my hand and 3" of rubber down below
No wings on my back but a rusted and bent halo
I threw out the good and ran with the bad
I have gotten over it and now looking back
The question is, am I happy or sad?

LUSTY GAME

Eyes connect as she slowly spins
No safe words can be used tonight
The game of lust is being played

Ankle bracelet and slender legs
Lips of crimson blowing a kiss
Whispering promises into the night

Upside down on the club's gold pole
Money floating down onto the stage
I watch my ol' lady play a lusty game

Montgomery behind me and Birmingham's up ahead
Going to get some Hooters's with the sauce so red
A little woman in short shorts with those big Ta Ta's
Bringing me a cold beer and drowning my wings in sauce
I like them hot, wet, and juicy through and through
Order me some half shells and buffalo shrimp too
Crisscrossing this country is my driving game
I always look for Hooter's, they have such infamous fame
One thing is for certain, beauty there always abounds
My beer is cold and the wings are always drowned
The food is always excellent I must agree
But it's the short shorts and Ta Ta's that do it for me.

No Clue

I have no clue what you will find in this diddy
Only hope that it leaves you feeling giddy
I could talk about pain or the loss of the mind
If I did, would you think I was wasting your time?

Instead, this will lead us to unnatural thoughts
Into the bliss of more insane and darker plots
Invisable death coming to you at an ungodly speed
The bugs ass hitting the winshield is what I see

I am a troubled soul who has lost his way
I have fallen from grace and bent my faith.
And I have never really tried to understand
What society deemed fit rules for this man.
The wastelands became my happy home
And as time went on my heart turned to stone.
Time always has a way of slowing us down
And as I age my views are turning around.
I'm on a new path to mend my ways
With the due's I've rang up now having to pay.
I feel the hell hounds chasing, closing in on me
But this dawg's still running and I remain free.

THIS TIME

Everywhere I look in the springtime
Things are born anew
The sunshine seems brighter
Flowers spring forth fresh
The scent of blood is in the air

Is where I'm going just where I have been
Can my shadow redeem my soul
I find only confusion

PEACE

The sky is grey this morning
Pouring down on me
Peace in mourning

SILENT SCREAMS

A View From The Soul's Edge

Section Two - Inside The Insanity

Come inside, and we'll take a ride
If you are willing
Peace is here but it's not clear
If it will be turned on today...

So sit back, and try to relax
Find out what I'm selling
The pitch is here so listen clear
Before you go on your way...

Come inside, and enjoy the ride
It starts nice, with pure blue skies
Twists and turns with false alibis
A storm is righteously brewing...

Silent screams will enter your dreams
Buckle up your mind for safety
Yes, please sit back and enjoy the visuals
Of these thoughts that you are reading

Insanity calls to you to open the third eye
Are you confused by what you're viewing...
Read deeper my friend, soon you will find
The reasons I scream while enjoying my ride.

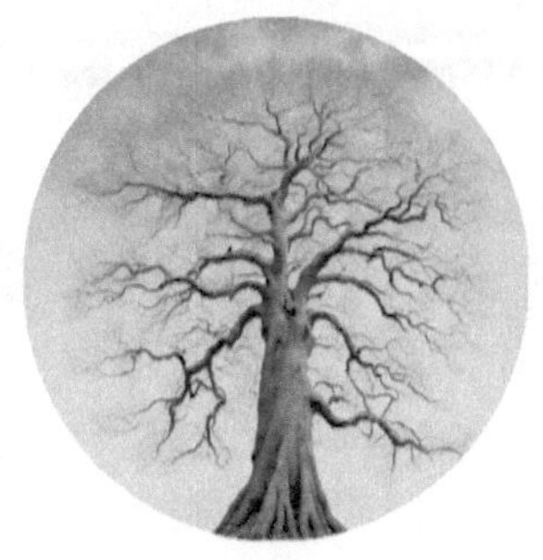

There's an oak tree in the park, its branches spread wide
It stands alone at the bottom of a knoll and weeps inside
The leaves are all gone now, it reaches out to the sun
The mighty oak waits on spring, for winter to be done

For years he has stood here, lovers have come and gone
Wearing scares on his bark, he reaches for the sun
Each year another circle appears deep down in his core
As the rings tell of his age he weeps as never before

The oak is proud and tall, as mighty as any tree has been
As leaves grow anew his beauty will shine once again
Still, the mighty oak longingly weeps for the time he sees
The warmth of spring and the loss of this winter misery

"HEADING WEST"

A whistle-blowing far away, I hear it loud and clear
Loneliness runs across my mind as I shed a single tear
California daze is coming back to me as if I never left
I'm off and running to you again. Yes, I'm heading west

The whistle-blowing is closer now, I know what it is
The feeling of peace reaching my heart, a simple wish
I want to feel the waves lapping at my feet
I need to breathe that mountain air smelling so sweet

I need to enjoy some redwood weed and big bear views
I want to lose these Mid-Eastern, bad-attitude blues
California bound, going back in time to re-visit my youth
Got to see you one more time, get to feeling smooth

As it is too fast and full of psychopaths, I'll bypass L.A.
Stopping in Forest Fall's where I can enjoy my stay
Maybe visit Shasta Lake, where I always felt at ease
California daze memories are returning once again to me

Newport Beach, where pretty women dig on those stares
Sterling Heights, a hood that guarantees you a scare
Orange groves produce smells next to a kissing booth
I want this feeling one more time, I have to feel my youth

I've got to get rid of these East Coast bad-attitude blues
If I don't, then pretty soon it will all be bad news
A whistle-blowing far away, I hear it loud and clear
Loneliness runs across my mind as I shed a single tear

I'm crossing the Mississippi, getting ready to sing
Pulling into St. Louis, I thought I would give you a ring
The number is still busy, I don't know what to do
Going to rock the city of Busch and dedicate this to you

We are rocking St. Louis, helping them to get down
When we're gone, they'll remember us rockin' the town
They pay the money because we are that damned good
It's a mutual love, things rolling like they should

As the smoke clears, I look out over the crowd
I take a moment to wonder where you are right now
Applause rings in my ears, you quickly leave my mind
We are rocking St. Louis, jamming one more time

Rocking the gateway of St. Louis with the help of K-95
The crowd is feeding us energy. What a time to be alive
The banks of the Mississippi, the gateway to the west
We're rocking St. Louis because St. Louis rocks the best!

How do you justify doing what you do for gain
How are you so happy, when you live in such pain
Won't say what's in your heart, who would understand
You are way too complex to be such a simple man

You get into people's hearts, then into their heads
You break their spirit, next thing, You've fled
How do you justify calling anyone your friend
How can you be so dirty and then do it all over again

Fast forward to rewind, it all seems to be the same
Is life to you something never bringing sorrow or shame
You are way too complex to be such a simple man
The next thing we know is that you've fled again

Yes, you are way too complex to be a simple man
Here we go brother, you have fled again
Please slow down and take in the sights you see
Take just a moment and explain yourself to me

Please take your time and don't flee the scene
Untangle the emotions, figure out what they mean
Talk it out with me and mine to release the anxiety
Understand you're just another of my personalities

Look into the cracked mirror
To see what you can see

Distorted truths of things
That could have come to be

So many unknown faces
They are all really the same

And if you stare too long
It will drive your mind insane

Visions from the cracked mirror
Install illusions in your mind

How can a person obtain
So many faces at one time

When they all at once start talking
It's time to get seriously scared

Visions from the cracked mirror
Attack you and leave you snared

When I was a child, I dreamed the American dream
Now that I am retired, I am still doing the same thing
Why didn't my teachers make sure I remained awake
I ended up dreaming my whole life away

Pursuing a life of luxury by working hard all day long
Night time came, and we partied until the money was gone
I don't know what happened to the American dream
I found the American wastelands instead; it sure seems

My wife was a mistress to sinful comfort for years
Alas, I left her in the dust, in a puddle of tears
Dreams are nightmares of a gentler vision in time
I like the ones that scare the boogieman's mind

A gypsy moth has things in common with me
We cruise from spot to spot to find what we can't see
Stop for a cool drink of water, then back on the way
I'm chasing false dreams through both night and day

When I was a child, I dreamed the American dream
Everything was possible, or so that's how it seemed
It took far too long to wake up and finally see
The American dream has levels of truth and reality

Now, when I close my eyes and go way back when
It's a whole different dream than it was back then
No longer reaching for unattainable ways to survive
The American Wasteland Dream is where I'm alive

White boy, you're not so innocent in your disgusting ways
We see through the naive bullshit and games you try to play
Innocence left you long ago when you were very young
So quit trying to make out like everyone around you is dumb

Life isn't the bowl of cherries they told you that it would be
Buckle up punk and quit playing these silly games with me
Depression isn't an excuse, as people deal with it every day
So don't express your sorry ass opinions to us in such a way

If I want to contemplate suicide it is reserved for me inside
Thoughts are all I have left that I have to hide
The skeletons inside my closet, right where they need to be
Secrets I've been told will go to the grave with me

The people I hurt in the past must decide what is right
I mean no harm and am filled with peace tonight
No one to blame for what I've done or what next I will do
Go back three lines to see if this poem was written for you...

Have you ever been on the ocean, looking at water so blue
Wondering if you ever saw land again, what you would do?
Ever sat on top of a mountain, smoking a joint all alone
Gazing out across the valley thankful to call this land home?

I've walked in the desert, hot sand burning my feet
I want to ask a question: is this what makes life so sweet?
Growing up in a city, too many people were always around
Being crowded by the masses can seriously bring me down

Forced to make quick decisions, mistakes at hand
Break out to the country, see the great divide again
Got to get away from the rat race, got to be my own man
I need to find inner peace soon, just as fast as I can

Two miles deep inside Mother Earth, felt totally at ease
Sat on a beach in the south, water lapping over my feet
I've listened to the roar of waterfalls, showers are so cold
Walked in silence on summer nights, answers quietly told

Fell three thousand feet with a chute, that's when your alone
The feeling of inner peace is what I call feeling at home
I don't need people crowding my mind all of the time
I like peace and quiet that only being solitaire can find

Sitting on a trussell
Just waiting on a train
Hearing that lonesome whistle
Calling out to me once again
Hopping in an empty boxcar
Let it take me out of town
They call me Hobo Billy
And I'm lonesome whistle-bound

I'll find some beans in Kansas City
Hope for a steak in Santa Fe
I sing the hobo blues every night
And listen for the whistle each day
I never see the family
No roots have I ever put down
I just found me a boxcar
To call my happy home

Hobo Billy is always friendly
No trouble do I seek
My shoes have holes in the soles
But I still have happy feet
My coat is worn and tattered
My hair is long and grey
I'll sing the boxcar blues tonight
As this bottle helps chase them away

Here comes the conductor
I know he is looking for me
Why can't they just let
Old hobos like me be
I know that if they catch me
I'll be jail-bound again
And so I keep singing these blues
Because they won't let hobos ever win

Everything I'm telling you is bullshit news
A hot start to living in the fast-lane blues
Sitting at the bar, Black Jack caught my eye
My Chrome .357 told him my good-byes

The back door opened and I turned around
I saw the star as I shot the next man down
Two men on the floor singing the dead man's blues
I realized it was time for my feet to quickly move

No time to wait on a slow-moving train
I got the blues and I need a fast lane
A Greyhound bus moves way too slow
I need an exit with no waiting to go

I hear that train whistle somewhere far behind me
I haven't slowed down, still fast on my feet
My reflexes are sharp, they haven't changed
I'm still blues riding out here in the fast lane

Someday somewhere, this will all come to an end
With all this running I will never be able to win
Through all these tribulations I've managed to stay alive
Living in the fast lane blues, I got hypnotized

The clear bathtub filled with bubbles instantly turned me on
When I walked into the bar and heard that slow blues song

A tiny robot dancing with you matched the bumps and grind
You were having fun on stage and truly blowing our minds

Tips passed from our hands to the little robot claw, then to you
After the set was over, we found a table for three instead of two

We talked in private a while all the time, not sharing names
Beautiful dancer earning a spot in my Stripper Hall of Fame

Champagne poured across your breast onto our waiting tongues
Two brothers and a dancer are joining in on this afternoon's fun

Yeah, two brothers bonding again in this fine afternoon delight
A sexy lady in a glass bubble bathtub is making us feel alright

*This poem was written in regard to an afternoon spent with my brother
Neil Shanebeck, bubbles forever bro.*

I once heard a story of a younger man's dream
I never guessed someone could be that damned mean
To rape, steal and pillage like the Vikings of old
To get away with murder, he would sell his very soul

He told of visiting cities both big and small
How he wanted to destroy them one and all
He said no mercy in his heart could be found
He wanted to burn the whole world to the ground

He claimed he had no love in his heart to give
Destruction and mayhem were his only reasons to live
Said that no woman could ever settle that man down
So he was destined to drift from town to town

As I sat there getting a buzz and trying to stay tuned in
Shutting out all sounds and concentrating on only him
His eyes were glazed over, and his words sounded so sad
How could someone so young be so damned mad?

Spring turned into autumn and winter soon sat in
Many moons have passed, here I'm talking to him again
His anger is gone now since old age has crept up on him
I'm happy to see he became a peaceful, loving man

Somewhere in his life, the rage turned stone-cold
With lots of stories that probably should not be told
So hush my mouth, I'll get quiet once again
Because as you see, I once was that younger man

Peeking through the looking glass
To see what I ought not to see
Wondering what in the world
Will ever become of me

Shuffling the cards of a worn tarot deck
An Ouija planchette is in my shaking hands
Trying to tell me where I must go next
Showing me a path I had not planned

Screaming that something is happening
The future will never again be made right
I continue gazing into that foggy crystal ball
Needing, wanting to find the answers tonight

A hoo-doo witch making me a scared mojo
Hiding it deep because it was not meant to show
A black cat running all inside my house
Superstition wins again...

I walked into hell late last Sunday
Gates were opened, and the lights bright
I saw a lot of souls in there that I knew
In the confusion, it didn't feel right

I looked around and saw the keeper
His toothless grin bore down on me
The music was rather soothing
Any kind of buzz you wanted was free

The keeper soon whispered over the blare
Announcing there was no cover charge
Then asked me if I wanted to stay there
He said the times were fast, but they weren't hard

I knew then that I had reached a crossroads
But I wasn't sure which way to turn
I looked inside to find the answer
All I found was a contract of terms

I broke that contract years ago, my friends
And I have been stumbling in the dark
Now I'm on my way to a new salvation
Coming back with a shattered heart

Yeah, I walked through hell late last Sunday
Hell, you might even say that I ran
Hell is just a narrow passageway
And Satan's always looking for a right-hand man

It's easy to get here, It only takes a second
But the one thing you must remember
The cover charge is your very soul
The music's loud, the lights a little dimmer

Everybody is having a grand time
It seems that it is never-ending
Until it desecrates your insane mind
And leaves your soul without mending

Why can't you hear all of that laughter
Everyone is eating their piece of the pie
We are not paying attention to the distant future
Have you ever stopped to wonder why

Looking behind you, you can find the answer
Buried somewhere deep back in your past
The answer might not be what you want to hear
But it will let you escape from hell pretty fast

Find the path you need to be on for salvation
The choice is yours alone to make
Will it involve the church of all nations
Or the party on the other side of the gate?

The volcano is starting to rumble
I feel the pressure deep down inside
Can't you see the lighting flashing
When you look into my eyes

Tremors will soon be starting
As anger clouds the mind
Tiny eruptions of violence
Will start the change this time

This volcano has laid dormant
For oh so very long
The gates of hell are opening
Calling me to come back home

I like the change that I am feeling
Evil power coming back again
With it a whole new laughter
A violent beginning to a mellow end

As the giant lay inside sleeping
Everyone thought I was so grand
But the nursery crimes are starting
And the lava is flowing once again

Inflicting pain is sure to bring me pleasure
As the tears roll out of your eyes
Satisfaction is but one small pleasure
As I come to take your lives

Published on SpillWords 4/2024

52ND AND NOWHERE LANE

The GPS isn't working, I guess I'm lost again
Closing in on 52nd and traveling on Nowhere lane
It should be a highway, as it's crowded to the max
People with no direction and lost in the past

The Sinclair dinosaur made more sense to me
Then, all these modern-day gadgets and technologies
Jobs can't be had if you are not computer-wise
It's hard to find half-truths in the hurry-up lies

Whatever happened to elbow grease and hard work sweat
Now it's all carpel tunnel and what's on the internet
Kids don't play outside. Do they know about hide and seek?
It's all about mobile phones and watching NetFlix next week

Look at the boomer parents and see where they are at
Thirty years ago, we were slender, and now we are just fat
Everyone is taking a piece of the pie, enjoying hell's bash
The whole world is Nowhere Lane, returning us to ash

So, 52nd Street, I need you to be crystal clear on this
As I head into the future with a single birthday wish
Life has been stuck on caution, put the world in reverse
Go back to the world we had before this technology curse.

Written on my birthday 2/2010

You closed your eyes and slipped into the night
A darkened fantasy would soon be taking flight
Into the void of an intoxicated mind filled with rage
The nighttime terrors were unleashed from their cage

Sweat broke out while in the throes of uneasy dreams
The night's host was to be Satan himself it seemed
The visions became crystal clear in the state of R.E.M.
You were earning points for committing mortal sins

You showed up all dressed in my favorite color red
After I had my way with you I left you for dead
Back out running in the heat of the night skies
You couldn't stop thinking of me kissing your thighs

The garter I removed with a graceful twist of the tongue
Opened up the game of reckless lust that we had begun
Sex-dripping juices flowed with such incredible force
You never achieved multiple orgasms like these before

After realizing that it hurt, you tried to get up and walk
You wished I was still there so maybe then we could talk
Sweat broke out on your brow and new terrors quickly showed
You thought you were awake but there was more dream to unfold

The visions became crystal clear in the state of R.E.M.
In visions of your dreams, a new fantasy starts to spin
This one starts with soft, silky wings that soar high above
Showing you that there is always room for God-fearing love

A path of gold will show you the way to salvation you seek
Teasingly placed before you so you could have a little peak
The path sparked flames, a roaring fire engulfed your mind
Blame it on the night sweetheart, you have run out of time

I once was a baby snapping turtle, making my way in life
If you got too close to me, you could be certain I'd bite
The winter time was closing in and starting to get cold
And nap time meant for me into the ground I would go

As I made my way across some man-made concrete
I was lifted into the air, off my scurrying little feet
In turtle language, I screamed as loud as I might
It was the start of this journey on a cold November night

Here comes that silly human, something new in his hand
I'll rub up against him as it might be a new toy again
Jump on the counter and give one of my merciful purrs
"Is he blowing me off, not rubbing my beautiful furs?"

"What is in your hand human pet of mine? I want to ask
What is that? I'll be right back, I'm gone that damn fast
Time me, lickety-split I can do a lap through the house
Now that I'm back, What happened to your ugly mouse?

Warm sand and water remind me of my birth on a shore
These plastic plants I try to eat make my tiny throat sore
I hide under this rock and patiently look for some meat
When I lock my jaw together on it, it is mine to keep

Ok, onto the rock might be a better spot to warm my blood
and shell
He placed a lid on top of my home and all I could think was
"What the hell?"
That furry giant thing keeps looking at me like a treat
That paw gets too close he'll see my bite can't be beat

You put my new toy in that glass with a lid my friend?
Oh it's moving, I'd best get into a crouch and be ready to
pounce once again
I love this game I play, a beast on the hunt for some bait
How do I get the lid off this maze of mouse fate?

Something has caught my eye and I must investigate that
I'll hit the sandbox thing and then go back to the rat
Humans not here so now is the time to carry out my
fantastic plan of fun
The lid goes off, my paw goes in and this is the end of this
pun

If there was a Santa Claus and I sat on his knee
Do you think St. Nick would grant my Christmas plea?
Wishes are granted for good deeds, how can he refuse
I've been good all year long, but I have got the blues

Down in the Big Easy, I spent some time with a friend
All I want for Christmas is to go down on her again
Being good in Alabama has got me nowhere real fast
Grant me my wish Santa, or you can truly kiss my ass

Santa please hear my Christmas plea
I know there are people a lot worse off than me
I don't want anything under the Christmas tree
I'd rather you grant us all, peaceful insanity

Fill my heart with eternal hope, I don't need any toys
I can't say I've been that good of a little boy
But Santa, as I believe you can plainly see
I need you to hear my private Christmas plea

Don't need a bunch of snow on the ground
It will be cool even, if no one comes around
Open my heart and let my soul be at ease
Santa, please hear this Christmas plea

A funeral found in the darkness of a closed mind
Is attended by sorrow and anger, raging with time
A detour was set up long ago in a violent storm
The road to reason is shut off from processing the norm

After losing a major battle on the field of insanity
Hope is nearly lost for the safety of humanity
A mighty warrior is born inside a defective brain
With evil and destruction, he is vigorously trained

As the powerful ocean, on the surface, he remains calm
Connecting with society like there is nothing wrong
While deep inside, a course of action is carefully planned
Hounds of hell sniffing out a path, for the death of a woman

Nighttime in Gotham City brings a madman's delight
One more chance to feed the dogs of death tonight
Leaving letters behind to taunt the police, I play my game
2000 fire incidents and six killings, gave me national fame

We've many things to discuss in this unfortunate task
How does one decide the right first question to ask?
Come in, lie down on this couch, and let's be stark
Do you remember when you first heard the dog bark?

This poem was written in regards to a psychiatrist talking to 'Son of Sam'

A jester sits alone in the dark
Streams of tears tracing his cheek
Memories of a life filled with pain
Shared as jokes to earn a living
A jester living in Silent Screams

He used his mind to run from the fear
Turning it around for simple applause
Laughter felt so warm and soothing
Beating away the pain and the hurt of life
The jester is alive in Silent Screams

Will he continue all alone and blue
A jester no longer making you laugh
Smiles erased from his heart and soul
He sits in the darkness with tears of salt
All that remains are his Silent Screams

Silver wings he dreamt of eluded him
The Army didn't want him because of his scaly skin
So he went back to his hometown
Feeling that life had finally let him down

He said that in life, he was dealt a losing hand
And had no choice but to become an outlaw man
Stand tall and proud, answer to no one
Living his life for the single sake of fun

Get in the way, and he will knock you down
These are the rules of life to which he is bound
Time in a cell became a common thing
He gave up on life's greatest dream

Live for today and take it as it comes
Everyone has to listen to their own drum
The beat of life can and will keep you down
Or you can stand mean and turn it around

The Book of Souls will someday be read
We all have to answer that call when we are dead
"Why did you do those things that you've done?"
Will be the question asked by our God's son

Lying in his grave, will sorrow consume him?
As it does in life now and then
Or will thoughts be found to be pure and true
Do you think you will be ready when this is you?

Hang my head because I didn't try too hard
I gave up and then I dropped my guard
I didn't pursue the perfection of God's way
Letting lust, greed, and temptation lead me astray

Dust off the candle and strike up a match
These 21st-century blues can kiss my old ass
Paid my dues and been down too damn long
Give me a Bass Ale, and fire up the bong

I don't care what the government tells me I must do
Rethinking old morals, bringing them back, round two
It won't be long before this soul is again feeling free
Yes, I'm looking forward to be back roaming the streets

It's time for a new Harley, and to don my old black vest
Let's put 'Dirty Ernie' back out on a new quest
When I let loose do you think that you can hang?
No longer be with Abel, but again running with Caine.

I'm not an evil person, but I've played the part so well
When the last curtain came down, it was hard for me to tell
One thing I know for certain, and this you must believe
When you run with Caine, the heart and soul will bleed

I quit running down the road about ten years ago
I laid back from society, thinking I was old
Times steadily fast changed, and the music did too
The 21st century has me feeling my youth

I want to take a ride, I'm tired of taking a break
Throttle in my hand, I'm leaving my life up to fate
Fresh blood in my veins, life's worries feeling lighter
If you want to ride with me, baby, hold on a little tighter

Boredom is just a state of mind, nothing you can't lose
Let's cruise the windy city and listen to some blues
We can ride to the Golden Gate, then head southeast
As long as we are riding, Life is all ok with me

I've traveled roads untold, searching for direction
Looking back into the past, I find no recollections
Let's travel through time and share a little space
Just give me good lovin' and honey, stay off my case

Growing up in the street, judged by everyone you meet
Gets mighty old after a while, but you still run for a treat
Living comes naturally for dogs, learning to survive too
People, you must listen to what this dawg is telling you

You can't catch a cheetah because they run too fast
And you can't cage love because it will never last
Dogs run free, sniffing around for an old bone
No choker fits me, so this dawg will not be coming home

Sitting at the track waiting for the fun to begin
Eating favorite treats and wearing that dawgy grin
Just like that a new lullaby is written for you to see
So hush little puppy if you please

Hush now puppy don't you cry
I'll ease your troubles with a lullaby
Now a puppy, someday you'll understand
That we all want and need the sandman

The sandman visits us every night
Placing sand in the eyes so you'll sleep tight
Lay you're little mind at ease
And hush little puppy if you please

Dream sweet dreams about meaty ham bones
With a side of Kibbles and Bits in a happy home
Chase your tale round and round in this dream
Mark that fire hydrant with a flowing golden stream

A circle of puppies all running and chasing a ball
The perfect dream is being played inside your skull
Your little legs kick and a bark is heard in the breeze
So hush little puppy if you please

I sit by this tombstone and play my music for you
The night passes by quickly as I enjoy what I do
I've never seen you but can never forget your name
A rose on your tombstone, I bet you drove the boys insane

Were you a pistol baby, or were you shy?
When you were little did Johnny make you cry?
Did you grow up lonely or die of a broken heart?
Questions without answers, we are so many years apart

I bare my soul to you asking nothing in return
Dawn is breaking so I'll hide while the sun brightly burns
When the moon starts glowing and darkness settles in
I'll return to play for you another love ballad once again

BLUE'S STEPPIN' BOOGIE

I married a woman fine as she could be
Two nights ago, she ran a game on me
Went through my money and then my credit card
Left me with an empty bottle,
As she drove out of my yard...

I got the Blue's Steppin' Boogie deep inside my soul
Baby took my wheels when she decided to go
The Blue Steppin' Boogie people in my soul
Has got me walking with nothing left to show...

She drove that damn chevy until it ran out of gas
Left it on the road with a note that said 'Kiss my ass'
I heard that she was not leaving this small town
I'm making it a point of not tracking her down...

I got the Blue's Steppin' Boogie deep in my bones
Baby broke my wallet and then broke our home
The Blue's Steppin' Boogie people in my bones
Finds me living in the tragedy of an insanity zone...

The neon lights will eventually show me the way
Where I can be happy in some smoke-filled haze
Until then, I'll move on in this broken-down life
Knowing that I am done searching for my wife

I've got the Blue's Steppin' Boogie in each step I take
The other half of me made a terrible and sad mistake
The Blue's Steppin' Boogie people in each step I take
Leaves her further behind by a great man ...
ah-whoo-hooooo   ah whoo-hooooo

I stepped into a wormhole to see where it went
And after ten hours my whole brain was spent
Illusions mixed with reality and opened my eyes
They by-pass the truth and fill the void with lies

They tell us how to vote and what we can say
To steal our freedom at any price they will pay
They keep passing laws to keep the poor down
They started letting Hollywood help run D.C. town

Greed has replaced morals and crime is the rule
We can rip them all off because the masses are fools
Like butter that is soft, hush money is spread around
From the POTUS to mayor's in every small town

They want our guns and freedom of speech taken away
They use the media to lie and try to get their way
Speaking of the news whatever happened to that
Now all that's on is drama and chewing the fat

Like a bad boil, it is time to clean this nasty wound
And clear all the crooks out of the important rooms
Fresh new blood is the way to turn this back around
To place this great country back onto solid ground

I walked into the county jail to start my bit
As a judge said, society had found me unfit
As that key turned to lock me down
I paused, to reflect on that lonesome sound

They wake you up hourly, so you can't get any sleep
The food they serve you isn't fit for a dog to eat
I look out my small cell window, just to pass the time
I see a house filled with spirits, liquor, and wine

Give up your life, I heard a man say
Once inside the system, it is where you will stay
In a two-bunk room measuring eight by six
Is where I'll stay until I am free from this shit

I mark each day as time rolls slowly on
Forty-one and a wake-up, I'll be long gone
When I hit those doors, across the street, I will go
Since a house of spirits is a friendly place, I know

I found myself on the back of a downhill slide
It wasn't what I expected to happen or to achieve
My feet out from under me, I can't seem to get a grip
The joy I had known turned to sorrow
Does anyone have an answer, I've run out of clues

I find the streets lonely and empty, dark in the sunlight
Is everyone taking cover and searching for higher wisdom?
The earth is spinning sideways, blue as blue can be
As I walk into the twilight of a new beginning

If I am going uphill in this human race
Why is gravity pulling me steadily into the curve
I find no accurate solution to the mystery I need to solve
My brain is tired of being stuck in a downhill slide

LEAVE THE CITY

I had to leave the city, or else I had to die
Crime and passion were the things that got me high
Rolling on two wheels, wind sweeping freely in my hair
I had to leave the city because I started to care

Fun and games, with raw sex on the lawns
I quit the city, and now those games are gone
I look into the past with both joy and regret
Good times and bad times that I never will forget

Dancers on my face and money on my mind
Waking up tired and running on three-quarters time
Stop at the clubhouse to see what is going on
Searching for that pigeon to be the next con

That is all behind me now. I've moved out of that town
I no longer care about who or what is going down
Staying out of the city is the choice that I have made
I handed back the patch and sadly walked away

Family is a concept I do not understand
Because I have always been a loner kind of man
I come from a tribe of medium size
All the family except me are wealthy and wise

I got off the beaten path and strolled onto a trail
When it came to doing right I always seemed to bail
I took off down the road not knowing where to go
I just seemed to drift wherever the wind would blow

Crossing this great country from ocean to ocean
Couldn't slow down I was constantly in forward motion
Highways and byways are etched into my brain
I've slept in snowstorms, sunshine and rain

I checked in with the tribe every time I'd pass through
And they would fill me in on whatever was new
All but one has passed into the great sky of love
And they watch me as they soar high above

So back to the Big Apple or on out to Shaky Town
If I'm not moving on, soon I'm starting to get down
A horse or a wagon it's all the same to me
I need to keep moving to keep my sanity

In the eighteen hundreds, I might have known fame
In this time and age, most people don't know my name
My horse runs on two cylinders and burns a little fuel
Back then it would have had shoes and been called a mule

One hundred years have passed and the cowboy became me
Now it's my turn to walk into a brand-new century
What awaits this cowboy in this new age of glam and tech
Because I'm damn sure going in thinking "What the heck?"

Our government has become a total disgrace
They took our freedom and slapped us in the face
Whoever decided that answers could go untold
Watching the destruction of America slowly unfold?

I paid SSI every week off the top of my pay
Now that I need it, no is all they seem to say
I've tried to take the time and understand
No sense can be made of their crooked plans

The fat cats of the government keep taking out of greed
Chop them off at the knees, that's what they need
Make them live more like the common man
Maybe, that's what it takes for them to understand

This country needs to open its eyes and look around
Continuing along this path is bringing us all down
Could there be a way to understand the dilemmas we are in
The Senate and Congress keep making these thoughtless sins

A revolution happened once back in 1776
They knew robbing them of their money was no fix
They fought for their freedom and fought for ours too
The time has come for us to see what we should do

Let's vote them out of office after just one term
Maybe then they would open their eyes and learn
Put the vote to the masses and not the elite few
Stop them from racking up all of these unpaid dues

It's not funny how they are destroying this great land
Making rules that only benefit their greedy hands
Make us feel proud to be Americans once again
By destroying the corruption of politicians' greedy plans

Confusion upon waking should have given me a clue
A foggy path turned, becoming a highway paved in blue
Potholes of mistrust leading into an unwanted zone
Leaving me feeling like Rae Doole in Black Snake Moan

I try to get it right, red flags appear out of the blue sky
I'm disappointed, to be honest, and can't understand why
Love is a funny thing, unexpectedly it turns lives around on
a dime
Trust, a fickle mistress, once again blowing my altered mind

Pylons push feelings into a line on this highway of blue
How many more people will I hurt before this trip is through
Will it matter after sleep has closed the door of today's pain
Is there any hope of getting back on the cloud of happiness
again?

Insanity grips the mind convincing me of wrongs I've done
My heart froze as black ice formed blocking out the sun
I look at the situation, confused more by a sea of self-doubt
And think to myself, do other opinions carry that much
clout?

I awoke and looked into the mirror one day
And I saw an old man where I used to stay
Paunchy gut, grey hair, and wrinkles under his eyes
These things might make another man cry

The old man who was standing there staring back at me
Made me realize how happy this old man should be
Stab wounds, gunshots, a total social disease
These things happened to the man gazing back at me

Not all life is bad, sometimes life treats me grand
Look inside your heart and you'll come to understand
Trivial things do not matter when time passes us by
Anger ceases to exist, with God's love you begin to get high

Days turn bright as spring comes back into my life
And without noticing happiness replaces strife
I remember days past when I had nothing to do
And I look into the mirror at the grinning old fool

Not all angel wings are gold and blue
There are angels with dark wings too
Although they still protect us from above
They are here to show us some tougher love

With tough love comes misery and pain
But it can show us the way back again
These angels with wings black like the raven
Can and will show us a way to get to heaven

Don't ignore these unique angels as they appear
Just like other angels it is good that they are here
Protecting us from the deal the devil will offer us
These angels have been known to fight and cuss

The Lord walked this path before we were born
He placed upon his head a crown of thorns
This heavy load was done to forgive our earthly sins
When he went to hell he knew his faith would win

Humans cannot afford to think we can repeat this deed
As the dark angel wings continue to flutter and bleed
Signs that they offer their help to ease us on our way
Our dues having been paid in blood on a long-ago day

And though we may stumble, we must try to emulate,
The love, the sacrifice, the peaceful ability to create.
Close attention must continue to be paid to the details
As dark-winged angels protect us from our own fails

Is your mind that far gone, or is this a game
Your questions about every word spoken feel lame
The facade you put forth for the public eye to see
Is it just an illusion of what you want us to believe?

Lost in delusions of a perfect world inside your mind
Have you been running around, wasting everyone's time
Take a moment and search in the depths of your soul
Learn to love yourself before resuming this false role

Hating the world for not bending to your every desire
Only leaves you in shocking pain, entangled in barbed wire
No trust can be shared, in a mind on a barbed razor fence
Sympathy won't be found if you sit there and reminisce

The world won't bend to your needs if you don't try
It won't stop and wait for another worthless alibi
The one way to get out of this brain-sucking trance
Is to revert to mayhem and start a new death dance

The dawn is breaking along the eastern horizon
I watch another sunrise and wonder what it is for
The heat will be coming, unbearable before too long
I know I should be going, but I don't want to go alone

The party was a good one, everybody had a good time
The mud is tasting strong with a shot of Irish wine
Terminal Island in the morning, Golden Bay by afternoon
I can be gambling in Reno by the fall of the new moon

The Radio's full of static, all those truckers talking trash
I have to get this rig rolling if I want to leave this place
Another five hundred miles are logged in the book
Another seven hundred driven is what it actually took

Two drops and a pick-up, and I'm under a new load
Heading back East, travelling these lonely back roads
A million miles behind me and how many ahead?
There's another sun rising, and I still haven't been to bed

I walked down the mountain to the valley below
What I was searching for I just did not know
I found a feather while I was walking on a path
Red with white speckles that I couldn't scathe

Further down the trail, I happened upon another find
India ink to record the thoughts of my altered mind
Ideas were forming with nothing to write them onto
I hurried back home having something I wanted to do

As I sat down and got ready to put ink on the quill
Tiny shivers of delight started giving me a thrill
Words came faster than I could ink them down
Soon pages of poems were found scattered all around

I awoke with a Silent Scream pouring out of my throat
Another dreamed-up illusion that started with a quote
The anxiety I started to get brought on quite the buzzkill
Until I once again got high with the thrill of the quill

Enough of this Tom foolery, knowing where this will go
Light up that roach, and then we will see what you know
Feel the burn between your fingers and thumb
Hold it for a couple of seconds, and the high has now begun

Blue Dream is working on my now altered imagination
Gelato helps to kickstart a new poetic creation
Words spun out of smoke, thoughts floating in my mind
Celebrating a lifelong love with Mary Jane one more time

Plant a seed, it grows into a leaf that eases the brain
Always choosing wisely when buying your favorite strains
Pray for the sun to help that green plant reach the sky
Little buds appear, bringing a mist into your gazing eyes

Watch your beautiful plant, and it will steadily grow
Removing bigger leaves, showing warmth to the buds below
A nine-foot-tall, bodacious plant will be the finished sight
With colas so full, glistening with trichomes in the light

Remembering long-lost haunts inside this quiet backroom
The pain I unleashed on this world, the souls I have doomed
Reflections of things that could only bring more pain
My mind reflects while I sit waiting on that black train

Those hellhounds never stop, behind me at every turn
Time to make them my servants or return them home to burn
I owned these hellhounds, I called them each by name
I sit here and reminisce, wondering where it all changed

They haunt their master, chasing thoughts inside my mind
Constant howling reminds me of when I wasn't so kind
Baying and barking scares people up and wide awake
Exciting me, wanting to move in the direction it takes

When turning over the coin of reasoning, you will see
The equation of truth and lies, is that hellhounds run free
And sooner or later, we all must face an uncertain gloom
But today, the train is leaving, and I need to exit this room.

I was out after dark where I did not belong
I heard the devil scream out an old blues song
I walked around the corner and saw a neon dive
I stepped inside to see that the whole place was alive

The sound I was hearing flowed hot inside of me
I forgot all of my troubles, I felt happy and free
Three dark angels were shaking their money-makers
No place for Puritans or their friends the Quakers

Step up brother and feel the music inside
Let it loose, I tell you that you've nothing to hide
Move your body to the bend of the strings
I said get up sister and shake your pretty thing

The devil played a solo on an old harpoon
The bass joined in and they tore up the room
By the time I heard the beating of the drum
I was catching a buzz and my mind was feeling numb

The house was rockin' no full chair could be found
Everyone was into what Satan was putting down
Dark angels distorting, the blues turned into grunge
The whole house was jamming, everybody having fun

Blues-filled grunge filled up the air that night
The atmosphere was ripe, it all just felt so right
Dancing the blues away until the sun brought a new dawn
I liked being in that neon dive where I did not belong

It was cold and lonely when into this world I came
In between life and death, I found laughter and pain
All the lessons in life define who you will become
The good and the evil total up the sum

Are the gates of heaven closed or opened wide?
Will I hang my head in shame or walk in full of pride?
I attended church today and did not feel at ease
Thoughts of lust made me feel like the devil's beast

This had me looking back at my past desires
Will eternity have me stoking the devil's fires?
I know here lately I've been tired and tried
For the feelings in life, I've buried deep inside

I've danced with the devil, I've been carried by the Lord
Heartbreak and happiness experienced on my own accord
Hallucinations can provide a clear view of the future
Which helps me be a good student and a better teacher

What I teach is often misunderstood or misread
It loses translation upon leaving my head
This understanding to you is what I need to convey
The joy of laughter and sorrow of pain is the price we pay

Have you traveled down the highway
Passing a hitchhiker on the side
Did you ever stop and wonder
Where he laid his head at night

Have you ever passed the homeless
That is left out on the street
If you have done this
Then don't you criticize me

There are people in this world
A lot worse off than you are
Take a look around to see
You don't have to search that far

Any town you find yourself in
Just open your eyes and see
And if you haven't done that
Then don't criticize me

Reach out to the lonely brother
Take an unknown sister by the hand
Open up your heart to them
Then maybe you will understand

Everybody needs a little help
It's not above your ability
And if you think it is
How dare you criticize me

Attitudes are contagious; I swear they truly are
The anger and the violence have gone way too far
Put a smile on your lips and pass a kind word today
Maybe if we do this, depression might fade away

Hippies had clues of how happiness could be attained
Without this, anger and hate are all that is to be gained
I don't know why we didn't follow this peace through
But it sure has changed the world for me and you

Take fifteen minutes each morning to find inner peace
If we all did that, our world could heal with ease
If something is not done to turn this awful mess around
Destruction and sorrows will bring this world down

Put love in your heart and spread it around really thin
If enough of us do this, then peace can be reborn again
Make a thousand happy wishes and pray for one to come true
This puts you on the right path, and it is such a simple clue

Newborn in the fifties, came out trying to shout
His elders telling him what Woodstock was about
Hanging out in an alley or someone's pad
Life was so easy, just share what you had

The seventies came quickly, just around the bend
All of a sudden it was us or them
Lid days were over, prices rose on the street
What were once friends were now customers to meet

The hippie rose and had their say
But in the end, the hippie had to pay
Peace in a pipe and flowers on the wall
After the death of the hippie, we see they had it all

People now out to make money or steal gold
The disco era entered and got mighty cold
The hippie sat back and watched the time go by
The Beatles were gone, no more 'Lucy in the Sky'

Society soon rode on its high horse of greed
Not comprehending the failures and ignoring heed
Society broke all the rules of love and peace
The death of the hippie brought chaos to our streets

The dwarf thought he would be brave one day
He climbed up on the bridge and started on his way
About a mile down the road, he found an old broom
Thoughts of a girl and then marriage as a groom

Later that same day, he came across a bear
He told him to look around and become aware
The dwarf blinked, and the bear went away
Jim Morrison appeared, asking if he could spend the day

He said that he was not afraid of the stars in the sky
The dwarf didn't seem to care to understand why
The dwarf held out a joint but backed up just a bit
He then asked Jim if he'd enjoy having a hit

Jim just laughed and turned back into the bear
He let out a growl to give the dwarf a scare
The dwarf shook and then held up a peace sign
This weed he was smoking was blowing his mind!

Secrets manifested in the soul, buried in time
Gathering in the recesses of a darkened mind
Life became a struggle as failures increased
A journey of hell traveled every time he'd sleep

Secrets of the darkness could bring mighty pain
If let free to roam among this world once again
Could the human race understand what this means
Would they blindly go on following worthless dreams?

Thumbs and fire put humans at the top of the chain
Random killing and violence became a winning game
Not enough to satisfy the evolving brain of humankind
Thus, beginning the destruction of our souls and minds

Robbing from Peter so that Paul can be paid each day
Making up new money so not only the rich could play
You can place it on charge, just let me employ a fee
Thirty-five percent monthly sounds about right to me

To recap what I feel deep down in the echoes of my soul
Humankind animals may be smart but they are slow
By the time they figure it out and try to turn it around
We will all be dead

Lost between two bodies of water is where I will be
When I decide to end this game of murderous glee
Until that time comes and I feel the urge to pause
Murder and mayhem will be left for your applause

Live at Five News will tell a story of horror so complex
It will scare you indoors and put your faith to the test
It starts up in Brooklyn, Maine, as I leave a head on a post
Continuing into Albany, a toll booth reveals a human roast

Not to be discovered in this maddening quest, I make a turn
Next stop NYC, where plenty of bodies will let me learn
Devising torturing techniques I can use in a different town
I take my time peeling your skin with no one else around

Everything tastes better deep-fried in the Deep South
I remove your tongue first, then tell you, 'Hush Your Mouth'
The remains of your bones are set against an old pecan tree
I see once again from Seattle as I watch a colored T.V.

Saltwater slaps the pier posts as the tide starts moving in
Tied down, you feel the fear when the jellyfish stings begin
Down into Los Angeles, another metropolis full of sin
I catch you on a bus alone, and the stalking soon begins

Small towns across the country offer unique tests of skill
I might have to begin the chase by slipping you a small pill
The gameboard of life is upgrading without time to pause
Speeding up the destruction of our earth for your applause

You watch the lightning, sounds of thunder in the night
Rain keeps the rhythm to an unknown song, feeling right
The wheels keep turning, taking us to another town
The little groupie beside me is truly bringing me down

She rattles on about losers and needing the right man
The groupies strung out, she could never understand
The tour bus stops for fuel, and smoke burns my brain
I find myself stoned again, singing in the rain

Tucumcari behind me, with El Paso straight up ahead
I should be sleeping, but I can't find an empty bed
So I grab another bud, toasting ghosts of stars gone away
To Hank, Waylon, and Johnny, may you have peace today

My partners in the band are putting up a mighty roar
I'm sitting here grinning as an ace hits the floor
Gambling, drinks, and fights make for a pretty good song
I'm staring at a pistol, knowing something went very wrong

Picked up a bottle of Beam, going to drink it till it's gone
Then I hear the click of the trigger and know I am done
To Waylon, Johnny, and SRV, may you have peace today
A flash of a muzzle, and another songwriter fades away

TIS' THE SEASON

I prayed for mercy to be placed upon my soul
As I placed you into your last chokehold
The pressure was applied and you were losing breath
Your lungs were gasping for something fresh

Tis the season for the lies to come to an end

As your lips turned a duller shade of blue
Our eyes locked and you realized that it was true
When I said that you would die a frightening death
On the day you decided to put my patience to the test

Tis the season to weep for another friend

Your body cooled down as you prepared to depart
My hands relaxed and I reached to check your heart
The beat was slow, faint, and barely coming through
The day of the dead was here and coming just for you

Tis the season to say goodbye again.

MR. EVIL

Once again, Mr. Evil is raising his ugly head
Telling me to put you inside a deep dirt-filled bed
To take the people you infect out of their pain
He's telling me to do this for him once again

You showed your true colors; what else could you do
You hurt many people and made even more feel blue
You ran your game and thought that you had won
I have an ace up my sleeve, and now you're under a gun

You see, Mr. Evil has long been a friend of mine
And I do favors for him from time to time
This here favor will please me more than him
I'm tired of seeing your false-believing grin

You've told me about all the lies that I'm willing to hear
You shouldn't have hurt one of the few that I hold so dear
So, mister, you better enjoy every breath
I will take them away as I bring you to your death

You were on top of the world, thinking you had it made
Thought you were slick with every game that you played
But you forgot, or maybe you were too dumb to know
If you want to win the game, you have to keep control

The one simple rule that you mistakenly overlooked
Made you lose the game, and now your goose is cooked
I'm going to be nice and take you down painfully slow
Because you messed up, and I want you to know

Mr. Evil and I are going to make you pay your dues
With your dying breath, you will know that you lose
Buckle up tight and get ready for your last ride
Because from me and Mr. Evil, you cannot hide

Don't try and talk your way out of this mess
Because you are a fool and flunked this life's test
After you are gone and all of this is through
Me and Mr. Evil, we might just visit your family too

Rubber melts the asphalt as we take another lap
Thunder roars in the ears as I bust another cap
Sirens start to scream, women they do too
Blood begins to ooze, taking your life from you

The money meant nothing, it was the principle of it all
You played a bluff without your back against the wall
The card you were holding that you thought was an ace
It was, in fact, a joke. Now you're dying and losing face

Me, I round the corner trying to exit damn fast
My heart quickly pumping as I scream 'Kiss my ass'
Now, Texas is but a memory, something from long ago
I'm sitting in Yankee land, watching it slowly snow

Thirty years in the bank, and you float across my mind
I just sit and chuckle. How could you have been so blind
I've been down to see you a couple of times since then
I'm exposing my soul, expunging myself of past sins

You were one of the first to corrupt my virgin ways
But you were a rookie, and for that, you had to pay
Life's a fast lane, got to know when to bust a move
Sometimes you have to fly low to avoid getting screwed

Crimes have been committed, for some I did confess
For the nastier ones I left behind no clues to guess
A box sits on a dusty shelf, answers never to be found
You have turned back to dust below that cold ground

I'm looking over my shoulder to see what is behind
I keep hearing the hellhounds barking in my mind
Your secret is safe with me as it has always been
My secrets drive me crazy every now and then

Listen in the distance, I've thrown them off my trail
Hellhounds barking but the sound is getting mighty pale
So again I rest easy, I've got more time to wait
Those hellhounds are lost and chasing more false bait

I hear the sound of crying down in the valley
I just turn my head and grin
You only live until you're dead
My savior is calling again

Murder is only a moment in time
My time in the South is over
I've paid the dues for the crime
I'm busting out of undercover

In the dark of mourning
The faces are haunting me
I long for the burn of sunshine on my brain
Why can't I open my eyes to see

Hallucinations are real if only you'd understand
I got a new sensation
And now that the words are over
And a new story awaits
In the dark of mourning

I hold the keys of Hells only gate

Don't you see the world has changed into a shade of grey?
The gates of hell were opened, and Satan has come to play
The gates were always waiting for the masses to arrive in tow
Most go in blindly, not paying attention to what they owe

I always kept my third eye open, when around those gates
I worked overtime to ensure that wasn't my fate
You see I've chased the pleasure of tasting lust and sin
Through it all, I managed to stop it from pulling me in

Looking through a fog-filled brain let me see clearly
That I stood to lose all of the things I've held so dearly
To turn around and face the consequences of my ways
Now is the time to be proud and done with sinful daze

The world spins into a spiral, it is losing control
Masses don't care about what happens to their soul
Most are looking for fortune, finding ways to survive
Walking into the gates of hell behind those sugar-coated lies

You don't see the world changing, Satan offers you free reign
The gates of hell are open, collecting souls at a steady gain
I watch you enter the gates that will lead you into sin
I collect your ticket as the gatekeeper once again.

Published on Spillwords 6/2024

The leaves are all turning brown now
A brisk wind is blowing in
Snow will soon be falling outside the window
Another misplaced summer is slowly coming to an end

Suzie was troubled at the beginning of the spring
Her life turned in the direction of disaster
How could the man she was in love with
Turn out to be such a cheating, lying bastard

She finds herself crying all day long
No hope, it seems, can be found
Her illusions have all deserted her
She has never felt this far down

Her man knocked her dreams out of the window
He made her feel so full of hate and shame
He refused to make sweet love to her
Teasing her became his favorite past time game

Suzie knows that the love has ended
She knows that she must move on
She has known no other lover
All her emotions have gotten up and gone

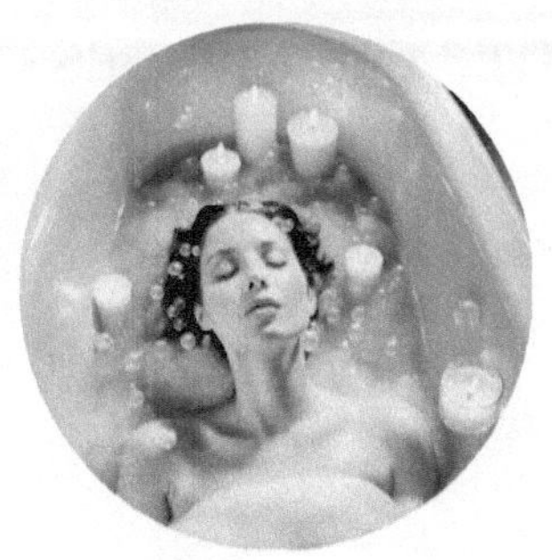

She finds a razor in the bathroom
Opens one more bottle of tasty wine
As the blood mixes with the water
She closes her eyes and lets her soul shine

Soon, she will be in total peace
No more tears will ever be shed
A tub filled with sorrow and wine
Suicide overtook the mind that bled

A young adult was shocked by trauma close to his heart
Found the gates of darkness standing open and wide apart
In daylight, it seemed like a logical choice to pursue
Options were available but the choices were few

Into the nighttime, he freely decided to enter these gates
His life was transformed into an unknowing fate
Life sped up, entertainment helped ease his troubled mind
Alcohol and drugs became his new favorite pastime

The crowded path became crystal clear in his mind's eye
The rules were simple, live in the fast lane until you die
Pills and wine slid down his throat without any regard
Emotions died out, replaced by a cold, hard heart

Fights and parties were everyday occurrences to endure
Loose women became his worst nightmares only cure
Ladies of the night wanting not too much in return
Hard life lessons he spent years being forced to learn

Staying in the darkness on the other side of those gates
He learned many ways of influencing other people's fate
"Let me show you how to have top-shelf fun"
"Snort that line and let's go play with these guns"

Wiser men and women stepped outside and turned back
Running for salvation and staying on that track
The longer he stayed the deeper he went to explore
He found in time he sold his soul like a cheap whore

A stormy night of brimstone fire lit up the darkened sky
Chains of the soul had him bound to an endless tragic lie
Searching his mind, he peeked at a way to get back home
Risky behavior behind the gates that was so well-known

The leader of hell had his mind on bigger fish to fry
Now, both lightning and fire danced across the sky
Close to the gates, he hoped to slide back through
And return to the realm of the righteous and true

Thirteen feet to travel and his soul might shine again
Nine feet now to be removed from the hell of righteous sin
A yard remains, and he can finally end this long harshness
But I enjoy being the keeper of Hell's Gates of Darkness

Welcome to the night train, enjoy this dark ride
Free entertainment awaits you once you are inside
Exclusive tickets, to all of your wants and needs
The cost of this ticket is that your mind will bleed

Running the rails, this train goes straight to hell
Come in, sit down, and enjoy listening to this tale
The bar cars are open and pouring mighty brew
Anything you can dream of will be served up to you

Forget your morals as they won't help on this train
Do what you want, You need help in going insane?
Picking up speed the night train rattles and hums
Collecting all the sins and adding up the total sum

Put that needle to use as you relax in that seat
Ease your pain with a variety of mind treats
No reason is needed to board this nighttime ride
All aboard this train where insanity rules with pride

My eyelids will not open, and my mind will not close
Lying here thinking about my troubles and my woes
The air smells stale while the time lingers on

And I lie here musing on darker things

Was yesterday done right or maybe I did it wrong
Either way, it's done and I need to remain strong
I guess I've got the time to think things through

While I lie here reflecting on vivid dreams

Judgment day will open my eyes to the gospel truth
And that day cannot come soon enough
This pine box bed is mighty damn rough

As I lie here entrapped in Silent Screams

Will there be a day when I'm totally numb
And these feelings of death will no longer come
Will I ever get back on my feet and try
To be a bread-earning normal kind of guy

The simplicity of how I'm living now
Has gotten me lost somehow
My brain is steadily spinning out of control
Fanasty, lust, and suicide are all I seem to know

I'm in a dreamland called Nightmare's lost
I have to find a way out no matter what the cost
Rewind only happens when in life you're stuck
And after some time, you just don't give a fuck

I say I'm not living, but just waiting to die
I'm stuck in neutral and don't understand why
In days of old, I was a lucky, fortunate man
I was always happy just being who I am

A smile on my lips, life was just too damn fun
But something went south and now I'm under the gun
Nightmares lost just make me want to cry
I need to wake up, I need to try

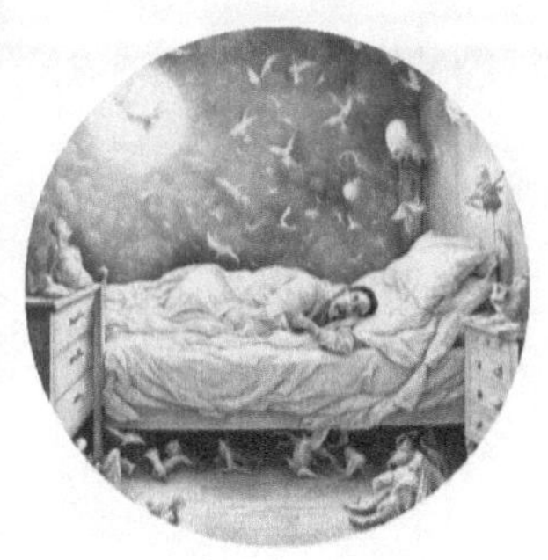

If I could find a way to love myself again
I might be able to leave this nightmarish sin
I know how Alice felt when the Red Queen went mad
Because nightmares lost has got me feeling so sad

Please help me wake up and escape this awful scene
Show me the way to get out of this wicked dream
Seems if I don't hurry and get my little light to shine
I'm going to be stuck in nightmares lost for a long time

When I'm gone, let me rest in peace
Laying up under some weeping willow tree
Whether up north or in Dixie land
You tell them all, here lies a contented man

I've never confessed to being right all of the time
This final sleep is sure to ease my mind
One thing that is easy to understand
You can tell em' all, here lies a contented man

Like the cowboys from the Wild Wild West
I've traveled the country, putting myself to the test
Pretty women, saloons, and ice-cold beer
These are but a few things that I enjoyed while I was here

A harvest moon to help me find my way
Untraveled paths to choose from every day
Watching the sunset across this beautiful land
Raise your glass in a toast to this contented man

Sookie Sue screamed out in her sleep late last night
Shaking and sweating, she turned on the light
She wrote down the dream so she wouldn't forget
This nightmare that woke her and had her so upset

Drifter Bob passed out in a cheap motel
Just another hard drunk night on the road to hell
He woke up feeling like he'd been hit by a train
The dream he remembered was driving him insane

Dreams interweave, and we call them Deja vu
How can I have the same dreams as you?
Frightened, we quickly open up our eyes
If you forget to wake from a dream, you die

Sookie Sue died in her sleep but left that note behind
Telling how the boogie man had raped her sleeping mind
Visiting in her sleep, her worst nightmare coming true
This brought the end of life to sweet Sookie Sue

Drugs and alcohol couldn't help Drifter Bob
He closed his eyes, and his heart started to throb
His worst fears surfaced, making his mind fearfully cry
Hellhounds in his sleep- that's how Drifter Bob died

Close your pretty eyes, and we will call this a night
I wish you sweet dreams and honey. Please sleep tight

This is the ballad of Jack & Doc
They were both locked down
But now they're not
Life in a cage and death staring them both in the face
This is the story of how they found peace and grace

In Indiana, Jack met Andy, and they fell in love
He helped Jack become free with a little help from above
Down in Alabama, Doc was drawing his last breath
And along I came to save Doc from certain death

Freed from the cages, fate would soon have them meet
To become brothers, both living happy and free
Loyalty abounds from deep within
Now, Jack & Doc run together through thick and thin

Believe this, if you see one, the other is not far behind
They spent their lives chasing each other through time
And so goes the ballad of Doc & Jack
Who both reside in doggie heaven just kicking back

*"This Poem is Dedicated to My Brother Andy and Our Dawgs,
Jack & Doc. R.I.P. to All Three*

I stand at the edge of insanity, waiting for pain to arrive
All this is happening and will leave not a soul to testify
The light is blinding while I wait for the shock to start
The result of carelessness will tear the world apart

Too late to understand how to turn it back around
Assholes ran this planet's way of life into the ground
Like the dinosaurs of old, our species will no longer stay
Questions not answered on this death journey today

Only seconds remain before my body returns to dust
A giant mushroom cloud of death is what is presented to us
I stare into a city of ruins as I feel the heat upon my face
It was only time until our species laid this planet to waste

Humans refused to understand the meaning of love & peace
Instead of spreading it around, they only made it decrease
Fighting over religion and who owned what piece of land
Brought total destruction to the race known as man

What happened to our future that we didn't understand
Why is destruction commonplace for the animal called man?
Through time, we record our mistakes and it's plain to see
Survival of this planet comes down to you and me

No simple cure to relieve Mother Earth of strife and pain
It will take a long journey to turn this around again
The animal kingdom watches as we destroy this rock
We need to come together to make this mayhem stop

Power resides in high places where bad decisions are made
To save this planet maybe we should make a trade
Let the not-so-wealthy take their turn at passing the plate
Maybe without the greed, we could provide a different fate

Seems like people without money care more about this land
Once again let's put the care of earth back into their Hands
I'm sure if they could talk the creatures of the ocean would
agree
Trash we are dumping in there is providing them with pure
misery

The common man doesn't take the time to think about things
We poison our planet without considering future dreams
You can see destruction we've done, knowing the cures to use
Turning this apocalypse into divine bliss means quitting all
the abuse

Destruction, death of this planet called Mother Earth
The animal called man is her last and final crippling curse
We need to stop now, laying this planet to waste
The animal called man is sending his trash to space

Published at Medusa's Kitchen 6/2024

In the clouds of mourning, we are drifters of the world
We watch the sunrise without registering the beauty

Down on the main street, life starts, and people move about
You see the filth that people leave behind as you walk by

Earth continues spinning, the human race isn't concerned
In the clouds of mourning, we are drifters of the world

We see things in perspective, and then we die.

I'm stuck in a rut with no place to be
I think suicide is the right answer for me
The people who love me show compassion all the time
But my true wish is that they leave me behind

My blood boils over, and my nerves are a wreck
I'm tired of this life, on that you can bet
You see, my life is swirling fast down the drain
I'm sick of living every day in this pain

I just don't see any reason to continue going on this way
I'm on a fast track to destruction, and that is where I'll stay
My mind is stuck in neutral, and I don't care anymore
So I think it's time for me to finally shut life's door

I can't say that life has been bad for me
It's at the end, and that's all I want you to see
There's no sense in touching on the happier times I've had
Tomorrow won't be as good as today, and today is really sad

Let me say goodbye and explain this poem of a rag
Life is not worth living while having a colostomy bag

I awoke to the sound of thunder, rain pouring down today
Awoke to the same revelation of being sad and grey
No destination in my future, not a clue from the past
My mind is caught in a whirlwind that will forever last

It seems to be the same old scenery when I gaze inside
I look hard for the answers, but the answers seem to hide
Life has forsaken me and left me with empty hopes
Every second of my waking moments, I struggle to cope

Looking at the past doesn't make any sense to me
Wasting time doing this; the future I will never see
To find a clue in the present, would I understand
How to eradicate these feelings and be a happy man

Dreams are everlasting, subconscious thoughts of the brain
I'm tired of dreaming, watching my life swirl down the drain
I can't reach out any further to people who say that they care
I withdrew from loved ones, leaving them feeling the Despair

Somehow, I must start living and again find goals to obtain
I've got to release the pressure that is driving me insane
If this is a lost cause and my life has reached a dead-end
I'll find a painless way to commit suicide, my friend

As I'm saying hello and goodbye at the same time
Feeling this confused should seriously be called a crime
I found religion to be tearing at the core of my thoughts
Heaven or hell, good vs. bad, is that all we got?

People are so strange in their everyday lives
Kidding themselves while they spread their little lies
Laughing, joking, and poking fun all of the time
Inside, hatred and anger are what hold the binds

Keeping those feelings covered with a false, thin veil
Nobody tells the truth because they think they will fail
Greed is found at the core of everyone
As so it passes on down to the daughter and son

You might want to be leery of someone's helping hand
They claim that they love you, but you don't understand
I can't understand who plays the greater fool
The preacher or the sinner sitting in the pew

When you are down, you find instant mistrust
Gossip is shared until all that remains is a big mess
Nobody likes drama is what nine out of ten people say
Just sit back and watch as they all head that way

You are stabbed in the back while looking into a smiling face
You stumble and fall, to compete in the human race
Who hurts the most, brother, foe or friend
Does it really matter come the day's end

Hurt is hurt; it is the sensation of sorrowful pain
People just love to dish it out again and again
The ones that you love seem to do it the most
"I'd never hurt a soul," they all seem to boast

Enough of this pain, and you start to withdraw
Soon, you start to wonder why you stick around at all
I leaned on you for support and no other
I'm sorry I was heavy. I thought I was your brother

Suicide thoughts running through my brain
If I go through with it, will I lose again
Bottle of Jack, morphine, and weed
I believe this is all that I need

Everything I own is in another person's hand
I went 360 degrees, and now I'm back again
Got burnt out somewhere along the way
All I have left is dues to pay

St. Pete is up there waiting on me
If I do this, will I need to plead
I'm not scared because I have nothing left to lose
Except for a full case of these empty blues

Friends will remember me with an easy grin
Because I was always good to them
And if you cuss me after I leave this earth
Peace be with you for whatever that is worth

I've run with the devil and the good Lord, too
I ran out of luck; I've got nothing left to lose
Don't bet a penny on me; don't waste your time
I'm out of juice and sitting here crying

Don't pity me for the life I have lived
I probably took more than I ever tried to give
I've been full of evil and full of good too
And if you knew me, you would know this to be true

I'm gonna miss Mama and my sisters too
But most of all, brother, I'm gonna miss you
I guess everything I've been trying to say
Is goodbye on this mighty sweet spring day

I have a feeling these blues aren't taking me very far
I need to get my head back into the medicine jar
I'm not living anymore, just waiting to die

I've been hurting for so long that I forgot my life's plan
The pain I endure makes me feel less than a man
I'm not living anymore, just waiting to die

Loved ones will tell you, I am just not me
I want to be the man that I used to be
I'm not living anymore, just waiting to die

I'm telling you, brother, I got lost on the wrong track
I can't explain because I don't know why
I'm not living anymore, just waiting to die

The blues have my mind in a terrible mess
I'm not finished yet, so on to the next
I'm not living anymore. Remember me kindly

I recently lost a lifelong brother, {Ronald Johnston} and this poem is dedicated to the exceptional love he shared with the world in this journey. All dawgs go to heaven, brother, until I see ya there, Bark, Bark

Silent Screams

A View From The Soul's Edge

Section Three - Edge Of The Abyss

Three squares in, and the mind turns on
Thoughts slowly start zipping right along
Giggles and laughter for no reason at all
Another fantastic Saturday night call

King Crimson's '21st Century Schizoid Man'
It will be leading me to another great band
ELP will provide the classic 'Karn evil #9'
Listening to these start to open the mind

Next, I let my ears focus on a Starcastle great
My mind floats away with 'Lady of the Lake'
I had to listen to the famous Bob Seger cut
Jamming up the stereo levels to hear 'Her Strut'

Mind trips don't last too long, it seems at the time
Music taking control of the visions in my mind
Six hours in the scenes continue to amaze
Not slowing down, I roll another one to blaze

Any journey opens the mind to contemplation
Next, I throw on the greatest of the Temptations
Tearing up the kitchen floor with dancing moves
I feel the 'Sounds of Silence' and fall into the groove

Spyro Gyra lights up the rhythm with some cool jazz
But soon, it gets hard with the great album Razamanaz
'Honey Hush, 'Stone Blue, and 'Mississippi Queen'
I'm enjoying this sound trip with visions, it seems

As I cruise into another 'Sunday Morning Coming Down'
I feel Jason Aldean in 'Try That In A Small Town'
Ending this mind trip, I place vinyl on the turntable of blues
Closing out with 'Day Tripper' on this three square cruise

A little mouse came in from the cold
He was soon following his sniffing nose
He scurried across the kitchen floor
He knew he had smelt that smell before

From the cupboard, he ran lickety-split quick
He went unnoticed, as fast as a clock's tick
He sniffed around under the kitchen drain
He couldn't find the cheese he'd come to claim

So he peeked out to see if anyone was around
Sidestepping the trap beside him on the ground
Over by the fridge, he again stopped to smell
Swiss cheese on rye was close; he could tell

Up on the counter, he spotted it sitting all alone
A month's worth of meals calling him home
How to get up there, he didn't have a clue
He had to stop and think for a minute or two

While he was thinking, he caught another scent
It smelled like chili with a rosemary hint
The little mouse knew that soon he must eat
This kitchen was slap full of tasty treats

LITTLE MOUSE

Over the chair and up the table, he did climb
Looking for a snack to satisfy his little mind
The table lay bare and the counter too far away
He had to make a decision and do it without delay

He got a leaping start and jumped into the air
He landed on the stove with half an inch to spare
The mouse was delighted, the buffet was now his
No sad ending here; the mouse took care of his biz

The green ostrich with zodiac eyes
Pulled his head out of the sand
He searched the nighttime skies
For an elusive constellation of man

Stars aligned and moved in motion
Other creatures were moving about
A gypsy moth was lost in devotion
And a midget tortoise started to shout

A nighttime chill was in the air
Leaves of longing, floating gently by
The gypsy moth wore a scarf of dare
And challenged those zodiac eyes

His green feathers instantly turned blood-red
Sam the midget quickly withdrew into his shell
I see the constellation was all he said
So the gypsy moth thought it was all cool

A new view for the longing leaves in the wind
But most of the scene remained in clear focus
Sam the tortoise was off and running again
Replaced by an orange-eating rabbit named Hocus

The ostrich returned to its color of bright green
Hocus pulled a bullwhip out from a hidden slot
The gypsy moth fluttered around without a clue
The crack of the whip and death became his last thought

A tale of old, a tale of new
A tale of riddles made just for you
If the moon was blue and made out of cheese
Could a purple giraffe cut the hair off of his knees

If the moon got mad and turned a deep red
Would it be time to get up, since we haven't been to bed
The river flows next week, it will be very grand
Three giant seahorses are leading an underwater band

The giraffe started crying and sat down in the stream
This riddle's all wrong is what he started to scream
Then, up on his lap, a wildebeest did climb
Listen up he shouted and I'll tell you all a rhyme

The mouse chased a cat in the middle of the night
The dogs all sat back and bet on the upcoming fight
The third baseman was safe and headed for home
The catcher had the ball, and the catcher was a gnome

Razor blades were found all strung around the place
Band-aids cover the purple giraffe's cut-up face
The dogs all ran away, and the cat climbed up a tree
No one was left but the mouse, the gnome, and me...

A tanned Impala came screeching up to the curb
A pink flamingo jumped on its back without a word
They were headed to the Savannah Street Jamboree
I hitched a ride because it sounded fun to me

A pride of lions stood outside the entrance gate
Collecting donations for the host Bonnie Raitt
Her slide guitar was kicking out some smooth blues
When I saw that familiar wildebeest talking to you

I knew right away he would leave unanswered tales
We have crossed paths before while sipping Bass Ale
Now he has started singing to Bonnie's sliding riff
Exhaling the smoke of nature's leaves, giving us a whiff

The jamborees just started, introducing a hot Saturday night
Two turkey buzzards are twisting to the crowd's wild delight
Over in the corner, sitting on top of a giant red mushroom
I whisper to a blue fairy and watch as she slowly swoons

Everyone is digging this evening's magical mystical tour
No one can resist the color of sound they find so pure
Bonnies' set is done, and next up is a saxophone-playing flea
From me to you, a fun night at the Savannah Street Jamboree

I saw a dragonfly moving a big oak tree
So I left reality to enjoy another fantasy
Upon my arrival, a wildebeest that I had seen before
Asked me if I liked his rhyme and said nothing more

I peered into a corner of a round room dimly lit
And watched an octopus perform an eight-puppet skit
Then a butterfly walked straight over to me
Strobe lights came on and changed the scenery

Thunder started clapping and rolling throughout the sky
I saw an elephant and an alligator staring eye to eye
Laughter erupted, and I turned around to see
I was on center stage, a turtle, a porcupine, and me

I had no idea what we were supposed to do
As I turned my gaze upon the crowded room
Every table I looked at seemed to be the same
We were stuck on lily pads in a red frog's evil game

The frog's tongue flicked out into the room-filled crowd
A chimpanzee started singing really deep and loud
The dragonfly was missed as he flew quickly around
I didn't understand the thought, and so I slowly drowned

The sun came out in the middle of the night
I awoke inside my dream, it was a terrible fright
A phone kept on ringing, but the bells made no sound
I was tossed into a box of lost and found

A yellow frog was kissing an old lamp post
Bella Lugosi was to be the night's host
Bella didn't show up by the time you arrived
To get out of this dream, I want to stay alive

With the fires burning, the flames got way too bright
I awoke inside my dream, it was a terrible fright
My eyes kept staring, but the eyelids wouldn't lift
Venus appeared before me bearing a thousand gifts

Her smile was lovely, and her attitude was so cool
I knew just what she wanted, I was not born a fool
I reached out to touch her satiny slender dress
The dream got cloudy, and everything turned into a mess

I screamed a scream with all of my lungs might
I awoke inside my dream, it was a terrible fright
When the clouds went away, my breathing did too
I needed to find an exit, but all I found was you

The lights turned dim and soon faded out of sight
I fell asleep in my dream, knowing everything was alright
Your arms went around me, and right then, I finally knew
To get out of this nightmare, I had to get away from you

Whisked into an unknown world
There was no exit, and my mind was blown
Animals were so strange because they had no names
Ice didn't melt but rather produced a purple flame

No horizon could be found to separate land and sky
Not a thing there was born and so nothing could die
What was sprouting out of the ground was not food
My mind fell into a daze. What was I supposed to do?

When I tried to speak, the words came out in print
So I sang a song until all my breath was spent
I then took the letters that hung there in the air
Scattering them about until I fell into despair

The letters became symbols that felt like Jell-O
When I ate them, they made me feel so mellow
I took a stroll to try and get my bearings
I came upon a tattooed cowgirl selling orange herrings

What came out of her mouth put true fear inside of me
Silent screams I heard, but I still couldn't believe
I turned on my heels and ran far, far away
I came upon a lake covered in a psychedelic haze

On the other side of that hazed-covered pink lake
I decided to rest and await my future fate
I laid down, and a vision zoomed in my mind with a zest
Awaking with my head laying upon your naked breast...
What a dream

Now I lay me down to sleep
Dreams I once again fear to greet
As I drift into a brand-new realm
My eyelids flutter, but I remain calm

I witnessed a turtle running by really fast
And a fat Queen bee served up under glass
How can a conch be seen upstream?
Because it can live in fresh water in this dream

The trees are all orange from what I can see
And caterpillars are stepping all around me
I hear the music playing somewhere, faint and far away
Sounds like some blues tune from a long-ago day

A team of mosquitoes went by, pulling a sled of cheese
Followed by a grasshopper saying Puff and pass, please
This is turning into quite amazing entertainment, indeed
Square dancing with a dozen psychedelic centipedes

Thoughts of men are filled with sin, and women always lie
The star of Jupiter shone down on me, and I will never die
The frog broke through the lake of glass
And from that day has remembered his past

An orange swan went to the moon to see what was ahead
I cannot die, I was never born, this can't be in my head
A sign on the left says the Twilight Zone, but I cannot go
I've traveled past the sun and went into a black hole

On the other side, life is old and man there does not rule
I rode a camel without a hump with a polka-dotted ghoul
I awoke and couldn't see and knew that I was blind
I fell off a shooting star and now drift through time

The orange swan flew by in a cosmic breeze
Saying something about gravity and pretty please
He was gone in a flash to be replaced with Saturn's rings
And a sound proposal from some strange being

Marriage is not an option in open space
How could I marry a three-legged camel without a face
The lustful sins quickly left in the cosmic sky
Thoughts of men are filled with sin, and women never lie

I stepped outside and looked at the sky
The sun was gone, and I had to know why.
There was a sudden flash that came without sound
And when I looked up, I saw down.

The path became black, and it started to snow.
The snow wasn't white as I knew it to be
But kind of mist green, and that puzzled me
The snow turned to mushrooms, and then they were gone

In this state of mind is where I belong.
The path soon ended at the edge of a cliff
And something was burning, so I took a big whiff
Roasted marsh mellow and brisket filled the air.

I fell into consciousness.

I ate a button and waited for the fun-filled ride
A giant grasshopper was soon to come cruising by
I jumped upon his back, and he took us on our way
Going to see a flea circus on this trippy kind of day

The grasshopper left when we arrived at the fair
A group of sea horses eating cotton candy just stared
I let out a giggle, and the scenery changed into 3D
I didn't need those special glasses to vividly see

A pair of red ants was dancing to unbearable sounds
That a drunken miniature anteater was putting down
On the stage that was colorfully lit with icicle lights
A band of renegade snails was setting up for the night

When I blinked my eyes, I witnessed a fantasy dream
Of a blue frog dressed in bananas and whipped cream
Croaking a song nobody had ever heard until that day
The grasshopper came by and asked if I wanted to stay

It was getting late when the snail band took the stage
The grasshopper stuck around, listening as they played
When the music turned to wine, I knew it was time to go
A mighty fine time with buttons produced a hellva show

I've told tales of old, tales of new, made shit up out of the
blue
Here I go again, trying to compose something good for you
The gnomes harvest green fields and pick mushrooms out of
shit
They cart it back to their castle, my mind has an imprint of
this

They work in a field of dreams, among skulls and other
Things
A fat lady is riding a pink pony down south of them a bit
Tigger staring at her ass while Pooh checks out a very large
tit
Deep down in the ocean below, Charlie Tuna has a mermaid
chained for show

At the top of the waterline, Duckman is having a time
And crazy Fritz the Cat, we all know where his mind is at
Around to the other side, surprised by what you see
A zipper running from the ankle up to the knee

Yosemite Sam is just a blazin'- I don't mean a joint this time
Eaor is lost in a tunnel, and Acme dynamite still costs a dime
Turmoil hasn't yet started, a graveyard up on the left
A crazy brick wall sits dead center on my cheat

An oak tree serves as a reminder of good and bad in the past
Boo-Boo adorns a spot above the stoma that serves as my new
ass
Angels protect the right side but need a little work
Miss Prissy caught Foghorn Leghorn and turned out to be a
flirt

King Louie is grinning while holding up the ground
On the right wrist, a rebel flag can be found
Somewhere on the skin canvas, cards and dice can be seen
Always more to think of, so let the inking begin...again

A ladybug flew in the door without paying the cover charge
She was looking for fun and planned on living really large
She scanned the room and found a table on which to land
She crawled into a drink and got buzzed listening to the
band

Four Beatles were on stage singing a song called 'Get Back'
Soon, the ladybug was in a dream, floating in a black flask
Inside the flask, there was another party raging on the scene
A feeding frenzy of sharks, leaving the remaining bones
clean

Nightmares turn around on a dime, and this one did just that
Staggering across the table, she found a bullfrog in a tophat
Flying while buzzed is only for the honeybees on this night
So she did what was best and danced to her heart's delight

The bullfrog dipped and spun her around on the table's edge
A pink elephant called her name and asked her for a pledge
When the dance was over, the house lights became too bright
Friday evening's masquerade ball became a ladybug highlight

She made her way back outside and flew into the night skies
Thinking about the awesome band she heard while being high
Drunk and disorderly, she flew in a completely straight line
Arrested by a lightening bug for night flying while blind

Epilogue

Exiting the Illusion

Only silence is left for reflection
Screams of the mind spilled out in ink
Peaceful insanity at the soul's edge

Thank you for journeying through these pages of my vivid imagination. With quill and ink, I wish to ignite a spark, setting your mind ablaze with images of the unexpected and opening your mind to life's endless marvels. Hopefully, the conclusion of Silent Screams leaves you both entertained and contemplative. Thank you for embarking on this journey with me,

Ernest Federspiel

About the Author

Retired and residing in Michigan, Ernest Federspiel is a seasoned poet whose writing journey traverses time. His poetry resonates with readers, exploring altered outlooks on life's realms of love and fantasy. Through his insightful and thought-provoking verses, Ernest invites readers to challenge the boundaries of the human spirit and soul. Prepare to be moved by the profound reflections and mind-bending imagery that define his journey of words.

Previous Publications:

Ink Stained Love
Released January 2025
Available at all major bookstores and online

Connect with Ernest Federspiel at
www.dawgydaddyresponds.org